O9-BRY-580

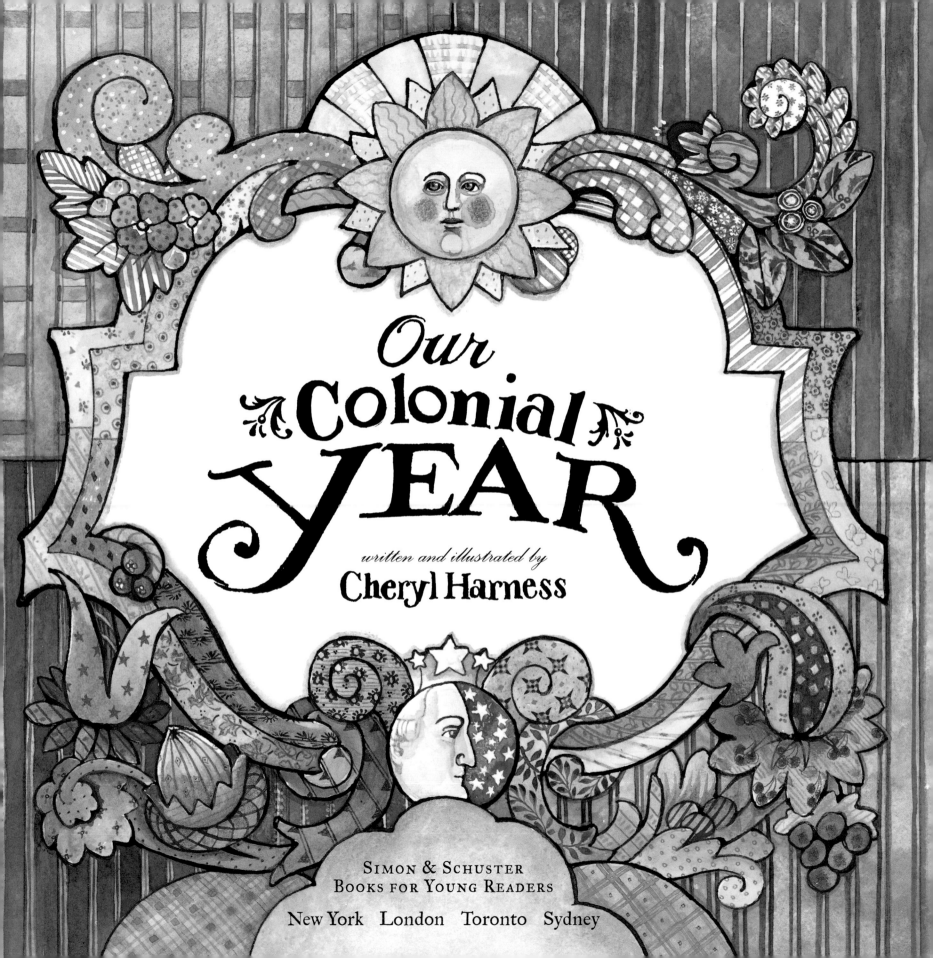

Our Colonial YEAR

written and illustrated by
Cheryl Harness

SIMON & SCHUSTER
BOOKS FOR YOUNG READERS

New York London Toronto Sydney

A Note from the Author

This trip through the Thirteen Colonies of British North America does not take place in a specific year. It shows how life was lived at a time when more and more of our ancestors were beginning to think of themselves as independent Americans. In their hearts and minds a revolution was taking place.

January

Women gather by the fire

when snowy winds blow.

Their needles fly,

their thimbles flash,

all through the winter day.

February

Folks tramp into the maple woods

through blue shadows in the snow.

They gather buckets full of sweetness

and syrup bubbles in the pot.

Massachusetts

March

The builders measure, saw, and sand.

They raise high the tall, oak mast.

Tap go their hammers, creak go the ships

along the dock in the fresh spring wind.

Rhode Island

April

The farmer, with his ox and plow,

turns the soil in the melting fields.

He gathers stones for sturdy fences,

and all the world is budding.

Connecticut

May

The flock is sheared; their wool is washed,

combed, spun, and dyed many colors.

Good, strong cloth is on the loom

and naked sheep *baa-aa* in the sunshine.

New York

June

Children in the fields and gardens

work in the warming sun

until it's time for games and play.

Then they run to the village green.

New Jersey

July

Men and boys work in the print shop,

make metal letters into words.

They press the type, all inky black,

onto paper white,

and people read in the summer evening.

August

Girls lead cows from the meadow

into the barn at twilight.

They sing softly as they milk and churn

in the summer mornings.

Delaware

September

Children gather slates and books.

The teachers clang the bell.

They troop into the schoolhouse

where they'll spend the crisp days learning.

October

Harvesters gather in the gardens,

orchards, vineyards, fields of grain.

It's time to pick, press, dry, and pickle,

when the leaves turn red and gold.

Virginia

November

Cooks scurry from cupboard to pantry,

from storehouse to hearth,

with bowls, platters, pitchers, and plates;

and all give thanks at the autumn feast.

North Carolina

December

Families talk and sing by the fire;

they read, they whittle, and sew,

thanks to wax and wicks and tallow

burning on a cold winter night.

South Carolina

New Year's

Townsfolk and travelers share the news

round supper tables at the tavern.

They make merry on a frosty night,

at the turn of another year.

The colonial year is fast away.

And tomorrow is an American day.

LAKE SUPERIOR

CANADA

Quebec

LAKE MICHIGAN

LAKE HURON

Montreal

Part of Massachusetts until 1820 when this land became the state of MAINE.

LAKE ONTARIO

N.Y. and N.H.

NEW HAMPSHIRE

Portsmouth

THE

LAKE ERIE

NEW YORK

Boston MASSACHUSETTS

Plymouth

THIRTEEN

PENNSYLVANIA

New York City

New Haven

Newport

N.J.

RHODE ISLAND

COLONIES

Trenton

CONNECTICUT

Philadelphia

NEW JERSEY

OF

OHIO RIVER

MARYLAND

Baltimore

Dover

DELAWARE

BRITISH NORTH

0 50 100 150 miles

AMERICA

VIRGINIA

Williamsburg

Jamestown

ATLANTIC OCEAN

NORTH CAROLINA

SOUTH CAROLINA

Wilmington

GEORGIA

ATLANTIC

Charles Town

Savannah

CECIL COUNTY
PUBLIC LIBRARY
301 Newark Ave

SIMON & SCHUSTER BOOKS FOR YOUNG READERS

An imprint of Simon & Schuster Children's Publishing Division

1230 Avenue of the Americas, New York, New York 10020

Copyright © 2005 by Cheryl Harness

All rights reserved, including the right of reproduction in whole or in part in any form.

SIMON & SCHUSTER BOOKS FOR YOUNG READERS is a trademark of Simon & Schuster, Inc.

Book design by Lucy Ruth Cummins

The text for this book is set in Historical Fell Type.

The illustrations for this book are rendered in pen-and-ink and watercolor.

Manufactured in China

10 9 8 7 6 5 4 3 2 1

Library of Congress Cataloging-in-Publication Data

Harness, Cheryl.

Our colonial year / by Cheryl Harness.

p. cm.

ISBN 0-689-83479-9 (ISBN-13: 978-0-689-83479-0)

1. United States—Social life and customs—To 1775—Juvenile literature. 2. Children—United
States—Social life and customs—17th century—Juvenile literature. 3. Children—United States—Social
life and customs—18th century—Juvenile literature. I. Title.

E162.H24 2005

973.2'083—dc22

2004016373

first
edition

E
Fic   Harness, Cheryl
HAR   Our colonial calendar

RIS